Love, Lust, and Passionate Desires

Abiding Love

CJ Millison

Copyright

Dedicated

To Everyone, That Has Ever Been Insanely In Love.

Table of Contents

Graduates-HS

Chapter 10: Double Whammy

Chapter 1

Paul and Gale

A passion so hot, it scorches the heart and alters the thought process.

Hi, I'm Megan, Gale's best friend.

Paul and Gale have had this hot, love, lust, attraction between them ever since Gale was a freshman and Paul was a sophomore in high school. They are so close that it's almost like they have a built-in radio signal that alerts them to the other's immediate presence. Gale and Paul described this feeling, "It's like a sharp, intense pounding in our chest, similar to a jackhammer breaking up cement on a sidewalk. Our hearts could not possibly beat any faster or they would explode into a million tiny particles. At times, we even become sexually excited just standing near each other, causing warm lubrication to ooze downward, leaving us wet between our inner thighs."

Perhaps, Cupid played a trick, giving them a double-portion of his magic potion.

Paul is so handsome, he has dark brown hair, and grass green colored eyes, they sparkle when he laughs, not to mention his muscular build that would turn most any female on. Gale has long, blonde hair, sky blue eyes, and an hourglass figure that keeps Paul longing for her touch

Chapter 2

Study Hall

This year Paul's a senior, and Gale and I are juniors. But don't let our young age fool you. The glue that holds our inner circle of friends together is that we are much more mature than most students our age.

Normally, we have last period study hall in the library. But today, the principal, and his assistant called a special meeting with several of the teachers to be held there. So we are being sent to the chemistry lab instead. The instructor for this classroom is required to be present at the conference since he has no scheduled class this time of day.

So guess what? The eight of us will most likely not be getting any studying done. Like an old quote that I have heard many times, "When the cats away, the mice will play." So true!

We are walking slow and in no hurry to reach the lab, Paul and Gale are cheerfully chatting away. In my mind, I am reviewing their past history as if I am watching a movie unfold.

Paul and Gale dated several times last year, but the passion was so intense between them that they knew the only way to be safe, would be to go on double dates together with friends.

Gale made the decision to remain a virgin for as long as

possible, but...I see their desire growing like a wild, ramped fire.

Gale is smart, she knows that after she graduates, she will have a better idea where her future will take her.

Paul has always made it plain to everyone that Gale is his...special girl. Even though, they gave each other the option to date other people, it rarely ever happens.

Paul is so comical. He is always sniffing the air around Gale teasing her, and sometimes he even howls like a wolf when the two of them pass in the hallway between classes. However, today is another story. As we walk through the entrance of the chemistry lab, we drop our books on the table top desks closest to the doorway. We are thrilled to know we have the next thirty-five minutes to cut-up and have a little fun.

There are eight of us total, and four of us are girls. The female group jumps up to take a seat on the black top counter that is typically used as a workstation to perform experiments.

The guys briefly pause at the doorway where they snicker and whisper in a teasing tone.

Paul is the first guy to step forth as he once again howls like a wolf, and with a manly voice he affirms, "Gale is mine, get your own doll!"

The other guys follow pursuit. As they walk up close to the workstation, they stop just long enough to pull out a chair

from some of the desks and
place them near us.
Within seconds, our attention
is captivated by the actions
taking place before us.

Chapter 3

Love and Lust on the Prowl

Paul pounced on Gale, like a wolf that just captured his prey. I see the wild lustful excitement gleaming from his eyes. They are already embracing each other in locked arms, as desire overpowers their brains.

I really want to stare...but, I try to disguise my curiosity by glancing back and forth at their acts of lustful passion. Paul is kissing Gale on her lower neck. Slowly he makes his way upward, kissing her tenderly up to her cheek, from there he moves to her hot moist lips. Paul's tongue enters her mouth as though they are making passionate love.

The remaining six of us sit quietly, we are encased in the action before us, as though we are watching a porn movie. I think to myself, a cold soft drink, and some popcorn sure would be nice.

Paul's left-hand now firmly clutches Gale's right breast. As my eyes scan this situation, I view Paul's private area gyrating around, then up and down, grinding against her right knee. Something has undeniably sprung to life in Paul's pants if you know what I mean. His erection is screaming to break free from his restricting slacks. They are gasping and moaning as if they are lost in a world of their own. To-be-sure they would not actually have sex right here in front of us, or would they?

Oh my! Paul's right hand is slowly inching its way up Gale's skirt. Within seconds, I see Paul rubbing Gale's inner mid-thighs as she begins to squeal with pleasure. Gales' need for him is more than she can resist, she is losing the battle of self-control.

But, before Paul could score home base, I announce with sincere advice, "Stop now! I hear someone walking this way." Paul does not respond to my stern advice, so I have to shake his shoulder to get his full attention. Once again I say, "Stop what you are doing and get to a desk pronto!"

What a fast way for Paul to lose an erection, it fell limp like a wet dish rag. Let's just say I saved the day and Gale remains a virgin.

By the time we rush to get seated where we had placed our books, except for Gale and Paul, they need a few recoup seconds to calm down. Mr. Wallace walks thru the doorway of the classroom. "I left the meeting early to check on all of you, but like I thought no one is studying. I need everyone to take out a book and get busy," he said in a displeased voice.

Gale and Paul are both seated by now, as they turn and look my way. Paul wipes his forehead like he is wiping sweat and they both whisper, "Thank you and smile."

Once again, they decide to keep at a safe distance but as we all know, it will be impossible. They need each other like we all need air to breath.

Chapter 4

After Paul Graduates HS

Just after Paul graduates from high school, he and Gale date every other weekend. They would love to see each other more, but Paul has taken a job at the local textile plant as a mechanic. He is also required to work two weekends a month to clean and repair the machinery since the factory is closed on weekends.

Paul works hard, trying to save some money. He plans to attend the local community college starting this coming fall. Paul's uncle promised him a job at his business firm if he would get his degree in Business Administration.

Summer break is over. So Gale, our classmates, and I finally have the honor of senior status at school. But, at the same time Gale is sad because she misses Paul. Truthfully, we all miss Paul's howling and teasing Gale as we change classes.

Paul has just started college and he is now working part time at the factory.

Gale and Paul's time together is short, but they make the best of every second they have together. Their passion for each other is blazing. It takes all of their willpower to fight off the desire to go all the way, as each second together is precious.

With hormones raging, and their need to be together, foreplay has taken them everywhere except penile penetration.

Chapter 5

Senior Prom

Senior prom is Friday-night. Gale, Sue and I informed our parents that we made plans to spend the whole weekend with some friends and classmates at the beach. We withheld the fact that there would be only six of us staying together at the beach house.

Paul and two of his previous

classmates from school named James and Don, chipped in together to rent the house for us. James and I will be going to the prom together, Don and Sue will be a couple, and, of course, Paul and Gale.

Sue, Gale and I had so much fun shopping for our gowns. We even went together to get our nails manicured and our hair fixed. This is such an exciting time in our lives, I think we will always be close friends. However, deep down we have mixed feeling about graduating high school which will occur shortly, although, it's exciting to start a new chapter in our lives.

James and I have just arrived at the prom. We carefully make our way to the designated area where our dining table is located. Seated at the next table, we find Don and Sue chitchatting with each other.

Of course, Paul and Gale are together, they are already on the dance floor. I can see the happiness beaming from their faces just to be together. Just now, they spot us sitting at our table. Gale motions for us to join them for a dance.

Even Don and Sue follows us to the dance floor. We all dance and party until our feet ache with blisters, in these new shoes.

The live band is terrific, but the noise is getting louder and louder, I barely can hear myself speak as I try to carry on a conversation.

After drinking one glass of punch I stop, because I am

positive it has been spiked.

Just as the prom is coming to an end, I agree to one last slow dance with James since I'm about to collapse from exhaustion. Then we bid good night to some of our other classmates.

The six of us leave the prom together, we are ready to make our way to the beach house.

Paul drove his SUV tonight, it has a third-row seat so we can all ride in that vehicle.

James and Don got

permission from the school principal so they could leave their vehicles parked on school grounds until Monday evening.

Don and Sue decide to take the third-row seat, so James and I take the second one. Paul is going to drive, so he and Gale get seated up front.

Just before Paul cranks up his vehicle, he leans over and passionately kisses Gale. We sense the lust that is already brewing on the front seat. While Paul is backing up and out of the parking space, Gale slides her left hand on Paul's upper right thigh. After Paul puts the vehicle in drive position, Gale starts rubbing and stroking Paul's right inner thigh, teasing him.

James is tall enough that he can see over the back of the front seat, so he keeps me informed of their actions. James whispers in my ear that the crotch of Paul's slacks is getting wet with desire.

Paul reaches over with his

right hand and tries to pull up
the bottom of Gale's long prom
gown, but he is unsuccessful.
Gale raises her body upwards
and slides her dress up to her
mid-thighs to please him.

He leans over while still
trying to steer the vehicle with
his left hand. Paul is now
teasing her as he starts to slowly
massage her left inner thigh
with his right hand, he inches
his way up to her womanhood.
Paul begins rubbing her moist
labia through her panties, and

soon she becomes wet with desire. Within seconds, Gale grabs Paul's hand as she squeals with ecstasy.

Paul lifts his right middle finger to his nostrils smelling her aphrodisiac aroma which literally drives him crazy-wild with a sexual rage. Paul breathes rapidly, he has no control over this burning lust that consumes him; he begs her to give him some relief.

Unable to drive the SUV in this state, Paul pulls over onto

the shoulder of the highway.
Paul is unable to speak a full
sentence in this condition. The
four of us sit quite, as not to
disturb them.

Gale unzips Paul's pants, she
eagerly slides her fingers
between the opened zipper
stroking his wet, slick,
manhood. Within seconds, he is
gushing with pleasure, like a
volcano erupting everywhere.
Paul's body jerks with
satisfaction as he groans and
moans, then he leans over and

kisses Gale.

Within minutes, we are back on the road, with Paul grinning from ear to ear as we make our way to the beach house.

Just before we approach the cottage, we decide to make a couple of stops, one at the supermarket for some groceries and the other to a beverage mart.

Before long, we are pulling into the driveway at the beach house. We are eager to unload our luggage and these supplies.

Chapter 6

The Promise

Paul unlocks the front door and swings it wide open. As we enter the house, everyone admires the lush roomy interior and the view of the ocean from the rear and side windows. We set the luggage down on the floor and turn back to go get the supplies and groceries.

After we stock the refrigerator and cabinets, we decide to check out the bedrooms and bathrooms. Don and Sue, James, and I, want Paul and Gale to have the largest bedroom and bathroom because this is a special night for them. They agree and thank us for letting them use the master bedroom.

I made a bargain with James early on that we might play around a little, but I am not willing to go all the way at this time in my life. James was somewhat disappointed of course, but I could sense he respected me for my decision. James and I are good friends, but nothing is written in stone.

We have no idea about the plans Don and Sue made, or if they even made any concerning sex, but that is their choice.

The best thing about this house is that each bedroom has its own private bathroom, now that's a plus for me.

I overhear Paul tell Gale to

stand outside the door of their bedroom until he can return from taking their luggage in. Paul quickly returns and gently but securely swifts Gale up in his arms. He carries her into the bedroom and he gracefully lowers her down onto the bed. Paul leans over her ever-so-gentle, he expresses his undying love and devotion. Then he kisses her tenderly.

Gale expresses her love for him in return, and then she raises up to set on the side of the bed. They sweetly smile at each other.

Paul gets down on one knee in front of her. Gale, "Will you please marry me tonight? We can have a private ceremony in front of our friends. Just think about it, we can say our own vows and make each other a promise to later say vows in front of a preacher or a justice of the peace. Even our families can be present for the ceremony after you graduate from high school. The six of us can make a pack and keep this service a secret until we can do it properly. I love you and I want to do right by you, but I need you now." Gale replied with bliss, "Yes, Paul! I will marry you now and once again when the time is right for us. I want nothing more than to be your wife."

Gale and Paul walk hand-in-hand back into the living room. Where they anxiously call a meeting with us. After explaining their proposal, we each make a solemn pledge not to reveal this secret until Paul and Gale say it's O K.

We each discuss who will take what part in the ceremony and we begin the preparation. Gale and Paul start working on their individual vows. James agrees to read scripture from the Bible at the beginning and then pronounce them husband and wife, you may kiss the bride at the end. The ceremony will take place on the beach strand near the edge of the water. Luckily the moon is nearly full and it's light gleams on the water to give off some light.

Sue and I want to surprise them and throw some rice afterward, to wish them good luck and abundance.

Gale goes into the master bathroom alone to shower and put her prom gown back on to use as a wedding dress. Paul uses our bathroom to shower and change his clothes.

Don and James carry a small table and a battery operated

lantern down to the beach strand so there will be added light to read the Bible Verses.

Sue and I get busy and prepare several cups of rice to throw at the newlyweds after the service is over.

Once Gale gets dressed she invites Sue and Me to help her with her makeup and hair. We also make sure Gale has:

"Something old--her grandmother's ring she wore on her finger to the prom. Something new--her new gown and high heels. Something borrowed--I lent her my pearls that I wore to the prom. Something blue--a small blue ribbon that we fastened in her hair." What a lovely bride to be, she is!

Paul waits in the living room for his future wife while James goes over (once again) the most appropriate scripture he could find to read from the Bible on this occasion. James chose the Scripture: 1 Corinthians 13:4-13. So when Gale is ready, Sue and I go and inform James, Paul and Don its time. We make our way down to the edge of the ocean while Don gets ready to escorts Gale to take her place beside Paul.

As soon as we see Don and Gale walking toward us...Sue and I start singing, "Here-comes-the-bride." When Gale steps close to Paul, Don kisses her on the cheek and he turns and steps back. Paul and Gale turn facing each other as they smile with joy.

James reads the scripture he chose. Then Paul and Gale take turns speaking their own vows of love, devotion, and promise, they even state, "Till death do us part." James pronounces them husband and wife, you may kiss the bride. As Paul and Gale turn and begin walking back to the beach house, we all throw rice their way.

James did a fantastic job as the officiating minister and Paul and Gale spoke such heartfelt vows.

As we all arrive back at the beach cottage, we toast the newlyweds, hoping they have a long, happy life together. Then Don locates a slow dance song on the radio so they can dance. We overhear Paul tell Gale as they are dancing, "You are truly mine now, forever and always." as he holds her ever so snug in his arms. I was just thinking out loud, "Isn't love grand?"

After their dance is over Paul once again lifts Gale into his arms and carries her to their bedroom.

Hearing their voices through the walls makes us feel as though we are intruding. So, Don and Sue, James and I, decide it time to leave the couple alone for a while.

So out the door we go for a stroll on the beach. It is so late, it's already three o'clock in the morning and we are utterly exhausted and needing some (zzz's) sleep.

We try to be as quiet as possible as we return to the

beach house. The sounds coming from Paul and Gale's room has James and Don turned on, and now they are trying to tease us.

I kiss James good night, but I make him stick to the rules and I go to sleep.

Chapter Seven

The Morning After

By eleven in the morning, Sue
and I were up before anyone
else, so we decide to cook
breakfast.

The aroma of freshly brewed
coffee and cooked food smells
delightful. Together we fix the
newlyweds breakfast on trays,
then we make our way to their

room. We gently knock on the bridal suite door to see if they are awake. With their approval, we enter the room and serve them breakfast in bed.

A couple of hours later the newlyweds walk in the living room hand in hand. Their happiness beams forth like a glow of sunshine.

Sue and I ask the guys if they would mind going to the supermarket for some ice cream and cake, since we did not get any wedding cake last night. Ha!

Ha! Sure enough, they fell for our plot to get them out of here for a while. Sue and I were actually hunting an excuse to talk with Gale alone. We are curious to hear what took place last night. So after the coast is clear and without much coaxing, Gale starts divulging the secrets of last night.

Gale's Description: As I recall after Paul carried me across our bedroom door threshold, he gently lowered me to a standing position at the foot of our bed. He kissed me ever so softly and then he turned my back to his chest as he wrapped his arms around me hugging my body ever so close to his. Paul spoke words of undying love and devotion forever. He stated once again that we would have another wedding service with our family present, and it would be performed by a minister or a justice of the peace when the time is right. Paul also stated that he actually feels that God has already joined us as husband and wife, and I agree with him. We just need to make it official by law.

Paul gently reached up and unzipped the back of my gown, then he slowly slides each sleeve down my arms so the dress will gracefully fall to the floor.

I turn facing him and I slowly unbutton Paul's shirt, sliding it off of his arms, as I kiss his neck. Next I loosen his belt buckle, unzip his slacks and unsnap his underwear. I become so excited as I watch his trousers and underwear fall to the floor. We both step out of our clothes that lay around our feet and slide our shoes off.

Standing nude in front of each other for the first time, we kissed and felt the warmth of our naked bodies touching. Paul reached up and cupped my breast, one in each of his hands, my nipples were so hard that they slid between Paul's fingers, arousing me more. Paul was so turned on as he stroked his warm wet penis against my flesh. My skin was drenched with his wet, lubrication.

Within the next few minutes, Paul lifts my body up and lowers me onto our bed. Paul bends down to kiss me as he lowers his body down and over me. His long, lean, strong legs press against mine separating them making me exposed and vulnerable to his need with my permission. Paul stated he would not impose any force on me until I told him I was ready. We kissed and caressed until, the heat between us was so hot that our bodies ached. Paul said, "I don't think I can wait much longer, I need you now." The burn of ecstasy was like a blazing fire that only we could put out. "I need you too, I'm ready," I said.

The pain was a sharp sting, but it was gone in no time at all. I am so happy we waited. We made love three times before day break and each time was more enjoyable.

I'm happy to know we are

married, but I know it's going to be difficult keeping it a secret from my family and others until we legally have marriage licenses.

Paul and I appreciate everything the four of you have done to make this time so special for us, and for helping us keep this a secret.

Gale's Description Ends.

Before long the guys return with the cake and ice cream. We enjoy our time together eating, talking and watching television.

After the movie ends we decide to go for a swim, so we put our bathing suits on and we grab a towel.

The ocean water is just chilly enough that we girls can't hide our hard protruding nipples from the guys, but they just joke as they delight in watching us.

It's a good thing that the sun is warm, so after we dry off with our towel, we can set on the beach and enjoy talking to each other.

Chapter Eight

The Weekend Continues

After returning to the beach house, we shower and change clothes. Then, we watch television and munch on snacks. As the last film credits are playing, we agree to make this last night here a special one. So after we discuss what to do, we all decide to go out to eat and dance at a nearby, well-known, local beach restaurant that has a dance floor and a live band.

Two hours later we arrive at the restaurant all dressed up. The atmosphere is charming and romantic, with live music playing in the background. This makes Paul and Gale want to announce that they are married to the world, but they know they must keep this secret for

After a meal of steak and seafood, we are ready to stretch our legs out on the dance floor.

James winks at me to let me know he has something planned. Not saying a word to anyone James walks ahead of us as he makes his way up to the band, he quietly asks if the next song could be a slow dance dedicated to Gale and Paul? The band members nod, "Yes."

After that song has finished, the lead singer for the band speaks to the audience. There has been a request, I will need everyone to leave the dance floor open to Gale and Paul only, for the next song. I wink back at James and I whisper, "That was sweet, thank you." Paul and Gale embraced and whispered words of love as they dance arm in arm.

I am so honored to be able to share this special occasion with them.

We dance and party until two o'clock in the morning, as the restaurant began to prepare to close, then we bid our good nights to the employees.

After arriving back at the

beach house, we are all exhausted and ready to get some sleep. I have a blister on my left heel from dancing, and I can barely hold my eyes open long enough to change into some night clothes. "Good night everyone, I'm going to bed," I say as my head hits the pillow. I'm so sleepy I don't even hear a reply.

Around four o'clock I am awakened by what sounds like the house is being demolished. I now realize that Paul and Gale must be having some rough sex because the headboard of their bed is pounding back and forth against that bedroom wall. Within three minutes, they both scream out together in ecstasy.

Just waking up I stretch my arms, as I turn to look at the alarm clock sitting on the nightstand I see it's already ten o'clock in the morning. I jump up from bed eager to collect a change of clothing and head for the shower. All of a sudden that aching blister on my left heel reminds me of all the fun we had last night.

That shower was just what I needed, I now feel refreshed and ready for a new day. I dry myself off, change into some clean clothes, wrap my wet hair up in a clean towel and put a bandage on the blister of my left heel.

I am so thirsty, so I decide to go get something to drink. Don is watching television in the living room and sipping on a cup of coffee. I smile and say, "Good morning." Don replies, "Hi beautiful." I've never noticed what a cute smile Don has. After fixing myself a glass of orange juice, I decide to put a couple of pizzas' in the oven for lunch. So, I set the timer and join Don in the living room. Don and I have never really had the chance to be alone so we could talk before since our other friends always seem to be around. We enjoy each other's company so much that Don asks me for a date the following

Saturday night. Don made the comment that he and Sue only went to the prom together as friends because they neither one had a date for that evening. So, I accepted Don offers to take the pizzas' out of the oven when the timer goes off. Therefore, I head back to the bathroom to brush my teeth and finish drying my hair.

By now everybody is up, so I head back to the kitchen for lunch. After everyone eats, we all take a seat in the living room,

James, Don, Sue and I joke around with Gale and Paul about trying to demolish the beach house last night. They laugh, and then Paul leans over and kisses Gale. We all agree to take a long walk on the beach and then head back to start packing for our return trip home. Tomorrow Gale, Sue and I will be returning to school and Paul, James, and Don will either be working or going to college. It is going to be tough for Paul and Gale to live apart and just date every other weekend. Their plans are to be legally married after Paul finishes college.

Chapter Nine

High School Graduation

The big graduation day has just ended with everyone throwing their caps up in the air. Now the hard part of bidding our classmates farewell. Paul has made plans to take Gale to the mountains for a long weekend as a graduation gift an extended honeymoon. But,

Gale's parents just assumed she would be going with a girlfriend on this trip.

One more year and Paul will have his Associates Degree in Business Administration, then they can have the wedding of their dreams. In the meantime, Gale plans to start the same local college as Paul and work on her teachers degree.

Being together for three days, and being able to have sex anytime day or night made this a real honeymoon for Gale and

Paul.

Gale returns home to live with her parents and she begins making plans to enter college this fall.

Chapter Ten

Double Whammy

Two weeks shy of Gale starting college, her monthly cycle is now three weeks late. With mixed feeling concerning the fact that they might be pregnant, they decide it's time to find out for sure. So, Paul and Gale went to the local drug store where they purchased a home pregnancy test. Unable to wait any longer for the results they perform the test in the drug store restroom together and...it's positive. They are happy and worried at the same time, how will their parents react to this news? How will they be able to raise a child and finish school? Decisions have to be made with the help of their parents and friends.

Paul and Gale make the decision to call their closest friends and classmates the ones that witnessed their private wedding ceremony on the beach.

They are hopeful that they will be able to join them tomorrow at Gale's home at six in the evening to break the news to both of their families. Everyone has been called and the meeting is arranged. Gale and Paul will announce their baby secret after their parents have been made aware of the private ceremony performed a little over a year ago. Both of their parents are curious as to what is going on.

Paul arrives at their home a little early so he can help Gale greet each person as they arrive for the scheduled meeting. Refreshments are available for the guest.

Each person arrives on time and after being served snacks everyone takes a seat. The parents start questioning the reason behind this social event? Paul and Gail along with their friends stand up facing them. Paul breaks the new about the wedding ceremony that took place over a year ago and about the honeymoon they went on to the mountains after Gale graduated from school. We take turns explaining just how beautiful the wedding was, as tears filled each mother's eyes. Gale's dad speaks up and says, "I just want both of you to be married legal by the law, you can see a preacher or go to a court magistrate and make it official." Both Gale and Paul agree that this is what they want to do. Now for the next surprise they say, "We just found out yesterday that we are pregnant and we need everyone's input on how we can work this out so I can finish school." Joy fills the house with excitement as both parents agree to help babysit as needed. The best solution that everyone could come up with would be that Paul should work part time and finish his Business Administration Course. Then, Gale can attend college for her Teachers Degree. Both parents decided to split rent on an apartment for them until Paul graduates next year. Gale even made the comment that she could find a part-time job for a few months to help with the bills.

They feel better now that everyone knows all the news. Paul's dad said, "Boy, that was a double whammy." as he smiled and hugged them both.

The next day they went to the magistrate's office and filed for a marriage license, and then Paul took Gale to look at apartments.

Three days later, Paul and Gale's parents, family, and

friends were all with them when they took their marriage vowels once again. Both father's each presented them with a thousand dollar check as a wedding gift. Gale said, "This money will also help us furnish the apartment that we found nearby the college."

They are so much in love that there is no doubt that this marriage will last.

Hoorah for young love!

Before you go, I'd like to say thank you for reading my book.